CONTROL YOUR TEMPURA

STREET FOOD COZIES, BOOK 5

GRETCHEN ALLEN

SUMMER PRESCOTT BOOKS PUBLISHING

Copyright 2023 Summer Prescott Books

All Rights Reserved. No part of this publication nor any of the information herein may be quoted from, nor reproduced, in any form, including but not limited to: printing, scanning, photocopying, or any other printed, digital, or audio formats, without prior express written consent of the copyright holder.

**This book is a work of fiction. Any similarities to persons, living or dead, places of business, or situations past or present, is completely unintentional.

To Nicki Kovacich Mech
I couldn't have done this one without you.

CHAPTER 1

Billie Halifax held tight to the railing of the fishing boat as it bounced over the Gulf of Mexico. Since her arrival on Sea Glass Island, she had been out on the water multiple times, but this was her first time out on a fishing vessel. The ride thrilled her, but she worried about the contents of her stomach as they moved further out.

"Are you alright, Miss Halifax?" Carl called to her from the other side of the deck. His dark hair was pulled back into a low ponytail at the base of his head and his slightly weathered, tanned skin gave him the appearance of a much older man.

"You need to get comfortable calling me Billie," she called back to him. "If you're going to run a food truck for me, you ought to get used to that."

"Okay, I will repeat my question then." Carl smiled. "Are you alright, Billie?"

She nodded her head. "I'm fine, but I'm not quite used to being so far out."

Carl Kensington moved across the bow of the large fishing boat. "Are you feeling sick?" he asked.

Billie shook her head. "Not yet, but I'm trying to be cautious since I've only been out on pleasure trips so far. This is a little different than what I'm used to."

"This is heaven to me," Carl said, gazing over the water. "But that's just because my dad was in the Navy. When we lived in Japan, we spent a lot of time on the water."

"Which is how you came to attend the culinary school, right?" Billie was still a little unsure of the details of her latest hire. All she knew was that he had come highly recommended by Alex Regent, the lawyer who handled her grandmother's estate. He was the overseer of her business interests until she proved herself with the fleet of food trucks her grandmother had left to her.

"That's what got me into preparing sushi, yes," Carl said. "My father loved the stuff, but he expected for me to go into the Navy just like he did, and my two older brothers did."

"That should have made him happy at least,"

Billie said. She turned to him and shaded her eyes with her hand. "Your brothers joined up."

Carl smiled and shook his head. "Not quite," he said sadly. "Right up until the day he passed, he reminded me that I broke family tradition."

"I'm sorry." Billie reached out and touched his arm. "I have a complicated relationship with my own mother as well. It's not easy, but, and I can say this because I have a good ten years on you, it does get better."

Carl nodded his head and turned his attention back to the water. Billie got the message that he was finished discussing the matter.

Either way, she was happy he had arrived on the island the day before. He had already proven himself as an asset to her staff. Enid Greene, the manager of her bakery mousse truck, had joined them at the commissary kitchen, home base for the food trucks, expressing concern over an event she had scheduled for the evening. The fridge in her food truck had stopped working, ruining the prep work she had done that morning for the event.

Right away, Asher Scanlan, co-owner of the commissary kitchen and the large festival grounds where it was headquartered, got to work replacing the fridge for her. Meanwhile, Billie had rolled up her sleeves and jumped in to help. The other trucks and their managers were busy serving regular customers out on the boardwalk and were unable to pitch in and help. Without an invitation, Carl had begun taking orders from Enid. In a span of three hours, the refrigerator had been removed and replaced with a new model and the cupcakes and prepared mousse had been remade. Billie glowed with pride when she witnessed a hearty handshake between Enid and Carl.

Asher, of course, had winked at Billie when they shook hands. He was dead set on the idea of two of her food truck managers becoming a couple. "Everybody's doing it," he teased.

"I think we must be about to our spot," Carl cut into her thoughts.

Billie noticed the boat engines slowing down. She watched as the experienced crew moved swiftly about. The captain, a large man in his sixties, directed the crew to release the fishing nets. Billie had met him a few days before through a mutual friend, the local police chief. She wasn't entirely convinced that the captain and Chief Abernathy were not related, at least as cousins or something. Both men could be doppelgängers for each other, though Captain Jacob Stephens was a shorter, more stout man.

The trip out on the fishing boat was born when

Carl had asked about including local catch on his sushi menu. Billie admittedly knew very little about the preparation of sushi and was happy to leave it to the experts. She gladly arranged for the trip on the fishing vessel, and the captain was more than happy to comply, given the fact that Carl had proposed buying the yellow fin, red snapper, and gulf shrimp directly from him.

The plan to use a local, fresh catch in his recipes was a marketing move to attract tourists and locals alike. Like the taco truck, wood-fire pizza truck, and the barbecue truck, the sushi truck would be parked on the boardwalk most of the time. During special events, the truck would relocate to the festival grounds, but Carl told her he anticipated only a few such events each year. Just last week, Nolan Wiggins, Billie's local mechanic and revamper of the old panel trucks she had inherited in her grandmother's will, had called to inform her the sushi truck was ready for business.

Unlike many of the other trucks, the inside of the sushi truck had to look a bit different. There had to be adequate counter space for preparation and cold storage for the delicate fish. No warming stations, grills, or other cooking methods were required. The prep work would be done each morning at the commissary kitchen prior to opening each day at eleven.

As soon as he arrived on the island, Carl had placed his stamp of approval on the food truck, designated "The Gulf Roll" with his input, and requested the trip out on the Gulf for the following day. He had promised to prepare a feast from his menu that night for Billie and Asher and any other food truck managers who cared to sample the delicacies.

Billie heard an odd grinding noise. She stepped forward and caught herself on the railing when the boat lurched slightly forward. "What was that?" she asked, looking over at Carl.

"I don't know," he said. "It could be that one of the nets caught on something. I doubt it was a bigger catch than the nets could handle, though, if that's what you're worried about. Some of those yellow fin tuna can get up to well over two hundred pounds in these waters."

Billie had considered the possibility that the crew had snagged a great white shark or some other undesirable creature, but Carl was right. The nets were made to hold many times that amount of fish. She could hear Captain Stephens barking sharp orders to his crew. Suddenly the whir of the winches sounded again.

"They must be pulling in the nets," Carl said, looking over at the activity in the middle of the boat. All the crew members were gathered around one of the large rigging arms that jutted outward from the center of the craft.

Billie and Carl stood close by and watched the flurry of activity. Suddenly, the movement stopped. A couple of crew members let out a yell and the captain sat backwards on the boat's edge, pushing his hat up on his head and frowning. He pulled a cell phone out of his pocket and began frantically scrolling through something on the screen. A second later, he tapped out a few words, then stuck the phone back into his pocket.

"That's it for today, then, boys," he said. "Secure that net and leave it just as it sets. Do not attempt to untangle things." He stood up and ran into the helm, and then pulled a radio receiver down from an overhead hook. He spoke a few short, fast words into the receiver and waited for a response.

"I wonder what's going on," Carl said.

"I don't know," Billie replied. "But I sure intend to find out." She released the handrail and headed toward the captain. "What's going on?" she asked Captain Stephens when he left the cockpit.

"Miss Halifax, I'm going to have to ask you and

your friend here to retire yourselves to the kitchen area down below," he said. His face had paled significantly in the last several minutes.

"Is there a problem, Captain?" Carl asked from behind her.

"Mr. Kensington," the captain said. "This is not business as usual for us, I can guarantee you that."

"The coast guard is on the comm," a crew member said. He poked his head out of the cockpit door. "Should we call the chief back on the island, too?" he asked the captain before handing over the radio to him.

"I've got this, Parker," Captain Stephens barked at the crewman. "You just see our guests down to the galley and make sure they are comfortable."

"Yessir," Parker said quietly. He stepped out of the captain's way and motioned for Billie and Carl to follow him below deck.

"Did something happen to a member of the crew?" Billie asked as they descended the steps.

"No, we're all fine," Parker said. He turned to face them. Like the captain, he was noticeably pale. "I don't know if I can say what's going on."

"Well, I really wish you would," Carl said slowly. He cast a knowing glance at Billie. "Because we're only here to observe things. I've just arrived to open a food truck on the island and was hoping I could buy directly from the captain."

"Oh, you can," Parker said quickly. "This isn't typical for us at all."

"What isn't typical?" Billie asked, her frustration growing quickly.

"We don't usually head out this way, so not only is this is a new area to us, but it's also…" Parker paused and opened the door to the galley and ushered them inside. He glanced up the steps before shutting the doors behind him. "Actually, folks, I'll be frank. It isn't every day that we snag a dead body in one of our nets."

CHAPTER 2

"A dead body?" Billie gasped.

"Hush," Parker warned. "There's no need to yell about it."

"There's a body in one of the fishing nets?" Carl asked in a quieter tone.

Parker glanced through the tempered glass window at the staircase again and nodded. "Yeah, and I've never seen one before."

"Are you sure it was a person?" Billie asked, careful to lower her voice.

Parker nodded. His face had regained a little bit of color and Billie wondered how old he was. He looked like a boy of eighteen or nineteen, definitely younger than Carl. No doubt the sight of a dead person pulled up from the water would have rocked him to the core.

"I know it was a person," he said. "When the older guys start to freak out, you know it's legit."

Billie's mind was reeling. "Could you tell if it was a man or a woman? Were they clothed?" she asked in a rush.

"Definitely a man," Parker said. He moved to the large table on one end of the room and pulled out a chair. "He still had his clothes. You could still see his bright yellow shirt."

"Parker!" Captain Stephens stood in the doorway to the galley. "I need you above deck, pronto!"

"Yessir," Parker said. He jumped up from his seat and headed for the door.

The captain turned his attention back to the pair of them. "I have to apologize for this, but I am afraid our little excursion is over for now. As I'm sure my crewman informed you, we pulled up something a little unexpected with the nets."

"Are we headed back to shore?" Billie asked.

"The Coast Guard is on the way here to investigate and indicated they would be in touch with your folks on Sea Glass Island," the captain said. "As a matter of fact, I just spoke with Chief Abernathy. He's working to arrange a ride for you two back to the marina right now. I informed him that neither of you had witnessed anything and he said it was best to remove any civilians from the boat while they investigate."

Billie nodded. "That's just fine with us," she said.

"I hope you know this is an unusual set of circumstances," the captain said to Carl. "We are very keen to supply you with all of the fresh caught gulf fish and shrimp we can, as we discussed before."

Carl smiled. "I'm sure that's true, Captain," he said. "Miss Halifax and I here both appreciate your attention to our business, but we can discuss all of that as soon as everything here is resolved. For now, we'll just pick up a few things from the fish market by the marina and touch base with you in a day or so."

Captain Stephens smiled. "Thank you," he said. "If you tell them at the market that I sent you, they'll be sure to treat you right. We're one of their main suppliers, so they'd better." He left them in the galley and ran back up the steps. The sea air must be good for older men, Billie thought. The captain took to the steps like a man half his age.

"Looks like there is some fresh coffee," Carl said. "Would you like a cup?"

"Please," Billie said. She would have preferred a glass of red wine but accepted the cup from him and sipped slowly. "Wow. I think sailors like strong coffee."

"That's my experience." Carl nodded and drank from his cup. "So, I guess we just need to sit down and wait."

Billie nodded her head and took a seat at the table. "I think that's all we can do," she said. She pulled her phone out of her pocket and began texting Asher. She wanted to let him know what was going on.

"I wonder if this is normal?" Carl asked after a second. "Finding a body in the water, I mean."

Billie wagged her head side to side. "I've been around here for about a year and yeah, things happen sometimes," she said. "But you have to remember, there are a lot of people coming and going around here. Even on Sea Glass Island, we get hundreds of thousands of visitors each year."

"Are you telling me that this place is dangerous?" Carl asked. "I don't mean specifically this place, but the island itself."

Billie shook her head. "I walk the island day and night. I'm not afraid," she said.

"Yeah, but isn't Mr. Scanlan your, you know, boyfriend or whatever?" Carl asked. "Doesn't he look out for you?"

Billie chuckled. "I suppose he does from time to

time, but I look out for myself a lot, too," she said. "Listen, I moved here from one of the roughest neighborhoods in Boston, and this is far safer than where I came from. That I can tell you."

Carl nodded. They sat in silence for a few more minutes. Billie finished her coffee and rose to set the cup carefully into the deep sink. She figured it was a good idea not to leave anything breakable on the table. They looked up at the same time when the sound of footsteps echoed just outside the door. The young crewman they knew as Parker had returned. "The captain said to come and get you guys. Somebody is here to pick you up and take you back to the island."

"Oh, good. Our ride is here." Billie waited for Carl to leave first, then headed up the steps behind him. When they reached the bow of the boat, she was surprised to see a large Coast Guard vessel anchored close to the fishing boat. She walked around the bow, breathing in the fresh air.

"Billie," Asher said from behind her. She turned and rushed into his arms before she could think about what she was doing. "Wow. Are you happy to see me or what?"

"I just want to get back home," she whispered to him. She was a little surprised at her own emotions.

"I'm over this way," he said and pointed to the other side of the boat.

"Happy to see you again, Mr. Scanlan," Carl said. He extended his hand to Asher.

"You can call me Asher." He shook Carl's hand.

"Whatever I call you, all I know is that I'm grateful to see you."

"Who told you to come and get us?" Billie asked, still in Asher's arms.

"Chief Abernathy asked me to find a boat and head out," he said.

"Who's boat is this?" Billie asked him.

Asher grinned. "Technically, it's mine now," he said. "I just made a verbal agreement with the owner to buy it."

"You bought a boat?" Billie asked with delight.

Asher nodded his head. "I figured it would be a nice getaway for the two of us." Billie noted a sideways glance in Carl's direction. "You know I'm going to take care of my girl."

Billie pushed back a little from him. "Why are you talking like that?" she whispered.

"Talking like what?"

"Like a teenager from a comic book," she said. "Carl is much too young for me or to be interested in me."

"Maybe I just want to make it clear that you're my girl," he said. He moved his hand to the small of her back, directing her across to the small boat waiting on the other side.

They followed him aboard. Billie took a seat on the stern and fumed. Asher had no reason to act so ridiculously macho, despite the fact that he had just come to sweep her off the fishing boat and take her home.

"Thanks for the ride," Billie said when they arrived at the marina. She stepped off onto the wooden dock the second Asher guided the boat into the slip. She didn't wait for him to tie off, nor did she wait for his hand to help her off of the boat. Instead, she walked straight down the dock toward the marina parking lot where her car was waiting.

"I'll give you a ride back to the festival grounds," she called over her shoulder to Carl.

"Hey, Billie," Asher shouted. "Wait up!"

Billie turned back around and raised her hand over her head. "I'll see you back at the kitchen," she said and turned to leave without a response from him.

CHAPTER 3

"Why do I get the feeling you're upset about something?" Rhonda Knapp, Billie's friend from the island asked her a couple of hours later. They were seated on a wooden bench on the boardwalk. Three of her own food trucks were parked less than a hundred feet away from her and she beamed watching the customers walk away looking like they'd just received the best food of their lives.

"I'm a little irritated," Billie admitted. She looked into the face of the older woman, who had been her grandmother, Adeline's, dear friend for many years. Sometimes, the motherly look on her face was just what she needed.

"By?"

Billie slumped forward on the bench. She watched the seagulls scurrying around her feet. "Asher," she said after a moment. She sat upright and faced Rhonda. "He came out to the fishing boat to get us, which I appreciate greatly, but just before we climbed aboard his boat, he started this macho crap about me being his girl and making sure everyone else knew it."

Rhonda threw back her head and laughed. "You're kidding, right? I would have paid good money to see that," she said.

"Why are you laughing?" Billie asked. "I'm really mad at him."

"Oh, I didn't realize you were that upset," Rhonda said.

Billie shook her head. "I'm fuming mad, if you want to know the truth," she said. "It was just so stupid. He had no reason to act that way in front of Carl or any of the other guys on board."

Rhonda looked at her carefully. "It's probably not my place to say anything, but Asher was burned pretty badly by his last relationship. I don't think he means to act that way, he just gets nervous."

She sat quietly for a moment, taking in the information. It didn't make things better, because she really couldn't stand jealousy, but at the same time, at least there was a reason he acted the way he did. "He has nothing to worry about."

"I'm sure that's true," Rhonda agreed. "But sometimes people have a hard time separating things. Asher is a good man deep down and I think you're the perfect woman to remind him of that."

Billie considered her barbecue truck manager, Dillon Frazier. He was at least a decade and half older than she was, smokey and grizzled, and much likelier to turn her head than a youngster like Carl. Even so, she barely noticed him. Asher was the man who turned her head, and she resented the fact that she had to prove that. But she did care about him, and she wanted him to know it and not have any reason to worry.

"Thanks for telling me about this," Billie said. She looked down at her phone when it buzzed. "Looks like Carl has his menu selections ready for us to sample. Are you hungry for some sushi?"

"Well," Rhonda said, standing slowly. "There's no time like right now to find out." She followed Billie down the boardwalk and back to the gate to the festival grounds.

They reached the grounds and headed into the

large, metal building at the center of the grounds. Billie went past Asher's office, not bothering to tell him the sushi was ready, and straight into the large expanse in the center where several kitchen areas made up the commissary kitchen. She walked right to the seating area that took up the rest of the space.

"Carl, this is my dear friend, Rhonda Knapp," Billie said when he approached their table. "She's a regular around here whenever we roll out any new cuisine."

"Pleased to meet you, ma'am," Carl said. He extended his hand to Rhonda. "Are you a fan of sushi?"

Rhonda blushed slightly. "I hate to admit it, but I've never tried it before," she said.

"You've lived on this island your entire life, and you've never had sushi?" Billie asked her.

"That's not so unusual," Carl said. "We're actually pretty innovative using locally caught fish in our sushi."

"I've never seen it served here," Rhonda said. "At least not in any of the places I frequent."

"If you're fairly new to sushi, you should know that I'm going to give you five different varieties, one at a time," Carl said. He set a small platter in front of them. "Traditionally, one uses chopsticks, but you can simply pick them up with your fingers."

"That's good news," Rhonda said. "I'm not very good with chopsticks."

Carl set several small bowls on each platter. "I'm going to give you a series of dipping sauces," he explained. First up is traditional soy sauce, followed by teriyaki sauce, and this is a small dish of wasabi. If you'd like a spicier experience, you can simply smear a little wasabi on the roll before you take a bite."

"What is wasabi, exactly?" Rhonda asked.

"Think of it like horseradish, but spicier," Billie leaned in and whispered.

"Oh, I like spice and I like horseradish." Rhonda smiled. "I'll give it a try."

"And this," Carl said, setting another small dish in front of them. "This is pickled ginger. I consider it a great palate cleanser between sushi rolls."

"Okay," Rhonda said. She made a face at Billie. "It looks like skin."

"Ignore how it looks," Billie whispered. "Trust me."

"First up, we have a dragon roll," Carl announced. "This is basically crab meat with gulf shrimp and eel, accompanied by avocado."

"Eel?" Rhonda picked up the roll and began inspecting it.

"Just try it," Billie urged. "You said you were going to have an open mind."

Rhonda nodded and picked the dragon roll up with her fingers. She dipped the roll into teriyaki sauce and then smeared wasabi over the top. She popped the roll in her mouth and closed her eyes.

"Wow," she said.

"Wow, good?"

Rhonda smiled and nodded. "Definitely."

Carl smiled and returned with another serving platter. He set the sushi on their plates and stood back to wait for their reaction.

"These look different," Rhonda said.

"That's because it's a nigiri roll," Carl said. "And this time, it isn't really rolled. Here we have some of that gulf yellowfin tuna on a bed of vinegared rice. Be careful with the wasabi this time, though. There's already a little bit of it in there."

Rhonda plucked the sushi off her plate and put it into her mouth. "Definitely spicy," she said.

"I think you have a new fan," Billie said. She picked up the printed menu he had given her and read over it. "I have to say, I like this simple menu. Good variety, great choices, and the inclusion of locally caught fish is an excellent marketing tool."

Carl pulled out a chair and took a seat across from them. "Not everyone in the sushi business thinks so, and we will still bring in plenty of fish as it is," he said. "But I don't see a better way to run a sushi truck on an island in the Gulf of Mexico."

CHAPTER 4

"How did the food tasting go?" Asher asked her when he knocked on the door of her tiny house later that evening. Waffles, her Tibetan Mastiff, rested lazily in front of the small sofa; his body nearly as big.

"It was fantastic, actually," Billie said. "Carl is a terrific sushi chef, and he knows how to incorporate the local catch into his food."

Asher nodded and tapped his finger on the counter near the sink. "It sounds like you've made another good choice in a food truck manager," he said.

Billie stared at him for a long moment then released her breath. "Alex Regent has a lot to do with those choices, but yeah, I think he will really excel at this," she said.

"Has he seen the truck yet?" Asher asked. His

attempt at small talk appeared painful. She could tell he was feeling uncomfortable.

"He saw it yesterday and he's there right now," Billie said. "He moved it to the right spot on the boardwalk and plans to spend the rest of the evening doing prep work in the kitchen."

"That's good," Asher said. He turned to look out the window, then swiveled back to face her.

"Look, Billie, I acted like an idiot earlier. I know you're a little frosty with me because of it, and you have every right to be. I just want to apologize and move on."

Billie swallowed hard. "Then do it," she said.

"Do what?"

"Apologize, and move on," Billie replied.

Asher's face was blank for a second. "Oh," he said at last. "I am sorry, Billie. I haven't had too many mature relationships before. And the one I did, well, it didn't end well. This is new, you're new. I mean, the type of woman you are, is new."

"What type of woman am I?" Billie asked suspiciously.

Asher shrugged. "You know, smart, driven, capable, smart."

"You said 'smart' twice."

"I guess that's the part that intimidates me the

most," he said. "Look, when you first showed up here, all I could think about was how you'd been given this golden opportunity to have a thriving business. Meanwhile, I had worked so hard for everything, and I didn't think it was fair."

Billie sat back, more than a little stung by his words. He really needed to work on his approach. "And now?"

"And now I realize that your grandmother simply gave you the same chance she gave me many years ago. She helped me out when I was about to lose everything, so how could I resent you for taking the gift she left you and running with it?"

He walked across the small living space and took a seat on the ottoman in front of her. "I saw you as a spoiled little rich kid getting another silver spoon, but after about five minutes of knowing you, it was clear that your grandmother had given you an opportunity you'd been denied all of your life. I've watched you grow this business into a thriving enterprise, and you're not even halfway there yet. You still have several more trucks to launch."

"Well, thanks. I appreciate all of that, I really do, but I need you to stop being so jealous when new people come around. I'm here, Asher. I'm not going anywhere, and I don't want anyone else."

He looked at her and sighed deeply as though he was letting out all the worries he'd been holding on to. "I acted like a big, stupid idiot because part of me is trying to catch up with the rest of me. My heart and my brain know I won the lottery meeting you, but my lizard brain still wants to act like a third grader whenever another boy comes around," he said.

"Carl is half my age," Billie reminded him. "Well, not technically, but it feels like he could be. He's a kid. I'm not interested in that."

"So, it's Dillon I have to worry about?"

"Well, there is that silver fox thing he's got going," Billie teased. "I'm kidding!" She reached over and kissed him on the mouth. "I have no interest in anyone else, okay?"

Asher nodded his head. "I am trying," he said. "Don't give up too fast on me."

Billie's attention was diverted by a notification on her cell phone. She picked up the phone and checked the screen. "I just got a text from Rhonda," she said.

"What, did she wind up with a stomachache from all that sushi?" Asher asked.

"Be nice," Billie warned.

"Seriously, what did she say?"

"She just heard that the victim from the fishing

net was identified about an hour ago," Billie said. "And an arrest has already been made."

Asher stood up. "Really? That was fast," he said. "Who was the person in the net?"

"His name was Sam Petrie," Billie said. "Captain Jacob Stephens was arrested for his murder." She looked up, shocked.

"But why?" Asher asked. "Didn't you tell me he was as surprised as the rest of the crew when the body was discovered?"

"He sure seemed to be," Billie said. She typed a message back to Rhonda. "Who arrested him?"

"What are you asking her?" Asher asked, leaning forward to peer at her screen.

"I wanted to know who made the arrest," Billie said. She hesitated. "Rhonda said it wasn't the chief or anyone local."

"Depends on how far out they were, but I think the Coast Guard would be in charge of the investigation," Asher said.

Billie's phone chimed again. "What now?" he asked.

"They identified the victim as a business partner of Captain Stephens." Billie set her phone down. "It sounds like he went missing a few days ago out in Tampa."

"Business partners? I didn't know he had a partner. I wonder if it's for another business or something?"

"I'm not sure." Billie stood up and opened the barn door to her bedroom.

"Are we taking this discussion into another part of the house?" Asher asked with an impish smile.

"Stop," Billie said. She tossed a throw pillow at him and pulled her laptop off the small table in her room. When she returned to her sofa, she opened the lid and searched the captain's name.

"What are you doing?"

"Seeing what I can find about the captain and his business interests," Billie said.

"What do you think you're going to find?" Asher asked.

"I don't know," Billie said. "That's why I'm looking." She rolled her eyes at him and returned to her search. The results showed a fishing company under Captain J. Stephens who owned a fifty-five foot long trawler dubbed the *Fin So Fast*," she read. "Was that the boat I was on?"

"You didn't get a look at the name?"

Billie shook her head. "I was more concerned about Carl and how he was going to take to everything," she said. "And before you start in with me again, the sushi truck was one of the easiest for Nolan to remodel and I want to get it up and running as soon as possible."

"Anyway, yes, the boat is called the *Fin So Fast* and Captain Stephens has been trawling these waters for as long as I have known him," Asher said. "I never knew him to own any other kind of business."

"Maybe he was a silent partner or just an investor or something," Billie said. "Still, it's weird to me that he would act surprised to find the body and then be arrested for the murder." She thought about how concerned he was with them still purchasing fish from him, but dismissed the thought as unimportant, at least for now. Business was business, no matter what and she couldn't fault him for not wanting to lose out on a sale.

CHAPTER 5

Billie woke early the next morning to walk Waffles along the beach. She had a busy day ahead of her and she had learned through trial and error, mostly error, that the pooch fared better on his own after exercising early on in the day.

For that matter, so did she. They walked along the beach just outside the festival grounds and headed in the direction of the marina. She thought about her conversation with Asher the night before, mostly about his apology to her, and realized she forgot to ask him all about the purchase of his boat. She wasn't even sure what kind it was, though she could easily rule out a catamaran or a sailboat. It looked more like a smaller version of the *Fin So Fast*, although it was missing the side rigging. Instead, there was a tall pole that was secured to the cockpit. She wondered if the boat had been some sort of fishing boat, but a private one instead of a commercial boat like Captain Stephen's had been.

She also forgot to ask him more about the interior cabin. During their trip back to the island, Carl had asked to use the restroom and Asher had directed him below deck. Billie wondered if there was any sort of overnight accommodation that she had missed. It could be that Asher hoped to do a little offshore fishing on his own. Or maybe he wanted to spend some time off the island and out at sea with her. She blushed thinking about it. The last thing she should be doing was thinking for him and putting words in his mouth.

Maybe it was a little bit of both. Who could say what his intentions for the boat were, aside from him? The boat may have been a purchase to help out a friend, or an investment for that matter. Either way, she was tempted to take Waffles for an extra-long walk to get a better look at it. She was sure she could find it again, but she decided the poor dog had already run his legs off and she still needed a shower before beginning her day.

A thought occurred to her when she made it back to the grounds. She shut the gate behind her and walked Waffles swiftly back to their tiny house on the far side of the festival grounds. The night before, when she had been searching for businesses owned by Captain Jacob Stephens, why hadn't she searched for businesses owned by the victim, Sam Petrie? That would have at the very least given her a place to start.

Start what, she wasn't sure, but since her arrival on Sea Glass Island, crime had found its way to her. And she had found a way to help the solving of some of those crimes along, even incidentally. Maybe she could help out with this, too. Not that she owed Captain Stephens anything, but the look on his face when he headed to the cockpit to call for help haunted her.

Once she was back at home, Billie tied Waffles to his outdoor cable and headed inside for a quick shower. She dressed and braided her hair over one shoulder, then picked up her laptop and headed toward the commissary kitchen. The kitchen had much better Wi-Fi than she had at home and Asher's coffee sounded like heaven to her at that particular moment.

When she stepped inside, she found several of the kitchen areas already occupied by several of her food truck managers. Dillon and his assistant, Olivia, stood side by side chopping up the brisket that had smoked in the outdoor smoker all night. Next to them, Enid whipped another large batch of chocolate mousse for her cupcakes.

"Do you have an event today?" Billie asked Enid. She set her laptop down on one of the tables in the eating area, choosing to hang out with the group instead of working in her office.

"Morning," Enid said to her. "And no, no event. We just all decided to open up on the boardwalk today to celebrate Carl's big day."

"That's right," Marcel Johnson, taco truck manager, said. "One for all, and all for sushi!"

"Speak for yourself," Isa Carello said from her station. She carefully spooned Alfredo sauce into a large tub.

"You're not a fan of sushi?" Dillon asked her.

Isa stopped and looked around. She nodded in Carl's direction. "What happens when someone gets bad sushi for the first time, bad enough that it puts them in the hospital for a day or two?"

Carl blushed. "Usually, they swear it off for the rest of their lives," he said. "At least that's what we were taught in culinary school."

"Well," Isa said. "I would be one of those people. It has nothing to do with you or the food you prepare, and everything to do with the sushi my mom brought to me one time when I was home from school for holiday break. That stuff was so bad, I had to have my stomach pumped."

"Yeah," Dillon said. "But given what we know about your mom, it wouldn't shock me if she got you bad sushi on purpose, just to keep you home longer."

Isa held her large spoon midair and stared at him. "You know what," she said, pointing the spoon at him for emphasis. "I had never considered that until just now, but you might be completely right."

"I don't mean any harm," Dillon said, suddenly self-aware.

"And I didn't take any offense to you saying it." Isa laughed. "I mean, the woman is certifiable."

"Wow," Carl said from his space. "That sounds like a story!"

"I'll fill you in sometime," Isa said. "First, you need to get to know me as me so you can separate the crazy from the daughter."

"Sounds like a plan," Carl said. Billie thought she caught a glimmer from Carl when he looked at Isa, but she wasn't entirely sure.

She took a seat at a table and opened her laptop, looking up in time to see Olivia carrying a mug of coffee in her direction. "Here you go," she said with a wink. "I figure you're in need of this after the day you had yesterday."

"Thanks, Liv," Billie said. She took the cup from her and sipped it immediately. Olivia turned back to the kitchen space and left Billie alone with her computer. She returned to the search engine and typed in Sam Petrie's name. Immediately, she found more results than she could begin to look through. She backed out of the search and added "Florida" to the mix, hoping to narrow things down.

Instantly, the results changed. She found a dozen listings for a recent obituary, apparently for Sam's uncle, and a handful of business listings. While she couldn't be sure the Sam Petrie she found was the same one that was found the day before in a fishing net, from the looks of it, the man had several business interests. She found a storage facility on the mainland, a small laundromat on the island, and a number of other, smaller businesses. She found a power-washing business, a leaf and debris removal service, and a construction company called "A-1 Enterprises."

"Hmmm," she said to herself.

"You look like you're intently caught up in whatever you're doing," Asher said. He pulled out a seat next to hers and looked at the computer screen. "What have we got here?"

"These are the businesses I found listed under the victim's name," Billie said. "I can't seem to find out whether this is the same Sam Petrie or not, though."

"Why not open a new tab and search the business names along with Jacob Stephens?" Asher suggested.

Billie smiled and typed in several combinations. "Bingo," she said a moment later.

"You're welcome," Asher teased. "What did you find?"

"A construction company," she said. "A-1 Enterprises lists Samuel Petrie and Jacob J. Stephens as owners."

"That may be the place to start, then. I'll help with whatever you need."

She looked at Asher, glad to have him on her side.

CHAPTER 6

Billie closed her laptop and put it aside for the time being. She walked to her office and picked up the calendar from her desk. With everyone in the building, it was a good time to review the upcoming events for the festival grounds. There were events that drew all of the trucks off of the boardwalk and onto the grounds, though they were few and far between.

For the most part, the taco, pizza, and barbecue trucks remained on the boardwalk, but in the case of an island-wide event, she preferred to have everyone close by. The businesses helped to promote each other that way.

"Have you got a second?" Asher asked her, interrupting her thoughts. "I wanted to talk to you about yesterday."

Billie frowned. "I thought we had this discussion last night," she said.

"Yes." Asher grinned. "But I wanted to talk to you about the boat."

"Oh, okay." Billie sat down at her desk and looked at him eagerly.

"Well, I don't know if you got a very good look at the boat itself, but it has a really sweet cabin below deck."

"No, I didn't," Billie admitted. She thought it was cute that he was mentioning exactly what she'd been thinking of before.

"Anyway, the reason I bought the boat is because I plan to move onto it," Asher announced. "I'm going to move out of my camper."

Billie was a little stunned. "You are? Why?" she asked.

"Partly because I've always wanted to live on a boat," he said. "Plus, there's a little more room than in the fifth wheel, and I think it's best for us if I move out there for now."

"Best for us? How on earth does this affect you and me?" Billie felt her anxiety skyrocket. Why did he want to move further away from her?

Their discussion was interrupted before he could

answer. "Hey, Billie," Dillon said. "Chief Abernathy is here to see you. Actually, to see both of you."

Billie pushed her chair back from the desk and stood up. She shot a worried look at Asher and followed him out of the office and into the hallway. The Sea Glass Island police chief stood at the end of the hall, waiting for them. "Is there someplace quiet we could go and talk?" he asked. He sported dark circles under his eyes.

"We can go outside, if you prefer that," Asher suggested.

"Fine, fine," the chief said. "Let's take a walk." He followed them outside of the building and around the empty festival grounds.

"What's on your mind, Chief? "Billie asked at last.

He cleared his throat. "First off, the two of you should know that I'm not here in an official capacity," he said. "Nothing I say here is as the police chief, and you don't have to tell me a thing. Clear?"

"Crystal," Billie said. "What is it you want to talk about?"

"You may not know this, but Jacob Stephens is my cousin on my dad's side," he said. "We grew up together, almost like brothers. He lived with us off and on all through school."

"That must be hard," Billie said, having already guessed they were somehow related.

"It's not easy," the chief said. "Even if this was in my jurisdiction, I wouldn't investigate it for that reason, but I do have some questions. I can't just sit back and let them throw the book at him."

Billie nodded. "What are your questions, Chief?"

The chief sighed. "I want to know what happened on that boat yesterday," he said. "I know your new truck manager was there with you, but I don't know him at all. I want to hear from you. What went on?"

"I didn't see the body," Billie said. "I was on the bow when they dropped the net. It made a really weird noise and then everyone started acting funny."

"When you say it made a weird noise, what sort of noise do you mean?" the chief asked.

"It sort of made this grinding noise and lurched forward," Billie said. "Almost like a stick shift grinding the gears. That's the closest thing I can think of to compare it with."

The chief nodded. "That's what I wondered," he said. "Did anyone act oddly or maybe like they weren't too shocked about it?"

Billie thought for a moment and shook her head. "The only other person we really interacted with was a crew member named Parker. I don't know if that was his first or last name, but the captain ordered him to take us below deck and look after us until someone got there to pick us up and take us back here."

The chief turned to Asher. "How about you? Did you pick up on anyone acting weird when you got there?"

"Honestly, Chief, I was only there for a few minutes," Asher said. "Billie and Carl were the only people I really interacted with. Everyone else was preoccupied with the Coast Guard at that point."

The chief nodded. "They've arrested my cousin and charged him with murder," he said. "But it doesn't make sense to me. Their case is basically that he killed his business partner over some reason they haven't specified to me yet. They say Sam was killed and dumped over the side of the boat by the captain where he normally fishes and then he went back to the same area and accidentally caught him in one of the nets."

"That does seem like a reach," Billie said, not really sure if she believed it or not. She didn't understand why he'd go back to the same spot and risk something like that. Then again, Parker had said it wasn't their usual area, so that didn't make much sense either. It was possible he dumped the body, and the surprised reaction was nothing more than an act.

"Where is he now?" Asher asked.

"In the county jail on the mainland," Chief Abernathy said. "I have to keep my distance, but I think he's being framed, and I don't know why. I know him as well as I know myself, and he is not a killer." The chief bid the two of them goodbye and headed across the sand to the parking lot.

"That was interesting," Asher said when he was out of earshot. "What do you think?"

Billie sighed. "I'm not sure," she said. "You gotta admit, it's a little weird that the captain's business partner would wind up dead in one of his fishing nets. I mean, when it comes to coincidences, how much more obvious can you get?"

"Right, but like you told the chief, the captain was as shocked as everyone else about the body," Asher said. "Then there's the whole framing thing. Who could have wanted to frame the captain for murder?"

"Yeah," Billie said with a sigh. "It's a little odd that his reaction was genuine surprise, but this entire situation is full of contradictions, it seems. If the captain killed Sam, why on earth would he dump him in a place he can easily be tied to? Especially when the chief said they think he specifically dropped the body there and went back. But if he was framed, there's no way he'd have known that was the spot where the body was."

"But you can't dismiss the fact that the victim was intimately tied to the captain, either," Asher replied.

"Did you notice that the chief didn't mention the relationship between the captain and the victim? He didn't indicate if there was an issue between them or not." Billie pointed out.

"Which could either mean that there were no issues between them…"

"Or that the chief simply doesn't know," Billie finished.

CHAPTER 7

Billie began the following morning with a walk of her own after she'd taken Waffles out. She planned to go toward the boardwalk so she could see each of her finished food trucks parked in a row.

"Take a look at that," she said to herself when the trucks came into sight. She looked at Taco the Town, Marcel's taco truck. She gazed down the road between the food trucks and kept walking toward them. The colors and designs of the exterior of the trucks amazed her. To her surprise, tears began to roll down her cheeks as she looked upon them. She smiled when she saw the mousse truck. Enid had certainly taken the concept and ran with it.

So far, each of the trucks was a thriving business of its own, including her newest, the pizza truck.

Recently, Billie had heard that mainlanders had taken to traveling across the bridge to Sea Glass Island at lunch time just for a slice of Isa's authentic, wood-fired Neapolitan pizza.

"Here's hoping sushi makes the same impact as the rest," Billie said aloud as she continued to walk closer to the trucks.

"Do you often speak to yourself?" Billie heard an unfamiliar voice from behind her.

"Who are you?" she asked the dark-headed man who came around and stood in front of her. "Please get out of my way."

The man shook his head. He was well over six feet tall and very large. "I'll move as soon as you answer some questions."

"Get out of my way!" She moved to the right, hoping to get out of his path. Instead, he took another step toward her.

"I told you," he said. "I'll let you go as soon as you answer some questions for me."

"I have no idea who you are, and I will not be talking to you any longer," she said. She turned around and headed the other way. She was closer to home than she was to the trucks. She walked three steps before the large man caught up to her. He stepped in front of her again, a lot closer this time, and frowned.

"Just do what I tell you and this will be over soon," he said. Billie turned to go back the other way, thinking maybe someone would be at the trucks to help her. He circled around her, once again blocking her from leaving. Panic filled her chest.

"Move!" Billie found her voice and screamed. "I don't know who you are, but you had better get out of here!"

"My name is Rob." Two meaty hands caught her by the shoulders. "There, now you know my name and I know who you are, Billie Halifax. I also need you to answer my questions."

"About what?" she shouted in his face and tried to break herself free from his grip. She looked around, seeing no one close enough to hear them.

"About a friend of mine, Trevor Kaufmann," he said.

Billie narrowed her eyes at the man. "I have no idea who Trevor Kaufmann is," she said. "Now, let me go!"

Rob shook his head and pursed his lips like he was about to scold an unruly child. "That's not good enough," he said. "You see, Trevor is a really good friend of mine, and he's also a friend of someone else you know, Captain Jacob Stephens. I think it's all pretty convenient, don't you? Especially since the captain's business partner wound up dead on Jacob's boat and nobody has heard from Trevor in several days."

"I don't know Captain Stephens," Billie said.

"Don't lie to me," Rob warned. "You do too know him. You were on the fishing boat when he pulled up that dead body."

"Being acquainted with someone is not the same as knowing them," Billie said. She tried again to wriggle free of his grip. "I was on the boat for professional reasons."

"I don't care if you were there to pop out of a birthday cake for a group of sailors. You were on that vessel," Rob hissed at her. His look terrified her.

"I was there, but I don't know anything else!"

"You know his cousin, Phillip?" Rob said.

"Who?"

"Phillip Abernathy, Jacob's cop cousin."

"I know Chief Abernathy," she admitted. "But until this moment, I had no idea what his first name was."

"Tell me why the chief was at your place last night," Rob demanded.

"No! You let me go now!"

Rob looked all around them for signs of any interference. "Listen, Miss Halifax," he said. "I am not the dude to mess with, do you hear me? Your sea captain…"

"He is not my sea captain," Billie snapped.

"Hush," Rob said, giving her a hard shake. "Captain Stephens is not who you think he is, and he is involved with guys like me. Bad guys. So, if you know more than you're telling me, rest assured I'll find out and you'll be sorry. Now, one last time, what do you know about the good sea captain and the body that was found? Why did the police chief spend so much time with you and your boyfriend last night?"

Billie felt a chill when he mentioned Asher. It was clear that he had been watching them. "Like I said, I don't know anything aside from the fact that I was on board when the body was discovered in the fishing net," she said. Tears streaked her cheeks. "That's the same thing I told Chief Abernathy."

Rob narrowed his eyes at her again and opened his mouth to speak. Before he could say a word, Dillon appeared behind him and struck him in the back of his head with his extra-large fist. Rob immediately released his grip on her and went to the ground.

Dillon walked around to confront him. "Billie,

run over to my truck and lock yourself inside," he said, not taking his eyes off of the man picking himself up off of the ground. "Call the police immediately and you wait in there with Olivia and don't come out or unlock that door, no matter what. Do you hear me?"

"Yes," Billie managed to say. She turned and ran to the food truck.

"Here," Olivia said when Billie stepped up on the small steps at the end of the truck. Olivia held the door open for her. She rushed inside and stopped only when she reached the far end of the truck. Olivia shut the door swiftly behind her and locked it.

"The police," Billie said, out of breath.

"Already done," Olivia said. As a former police officer herself, Billie wasn't surprised she had already made the call. "I happened to step outside and saw you and that guy. I told Dillon right away and then called."

Billie nodded her head. The tears flowed harder.

"You're safe now," Olivia said. Billie raised her head and looked at her. "What happened?

Billie inhaled sharply and wiped her eyes. "I don't know."

"Any idea who he is?" Olivia asked after a moment. Outside they heard shouts and cursing, but it was difficult to see what was actually going on from inside the truck.

She shook her head quickly. "He has something to do with a guy he claims knows the boat captain they arrested," she said. "He claims another guy the captain knew has gone missing as well."

"Huh," Olivia said. "That's weird. Did he say anything else?"

"Aside from threatening me? He said he was a bad dude, and that Captain Stephens is, too."

"Did he hurt you?" Olivia asked.

Billie shook her head. "Aside from digging his fingers into my shoulders, no," she said. "Not really." Her shoulders still ached.

"Move your shirt over," she ordered. Billie moved the collar of her t-shirt to the side with her free hand.

"Oh, man." Olivia immediately frowned.

"What is it?" Billie asked.

"You're a little red," Olivia said.

Billie nodded. "Tell me about it," she said. They heard the wail of the police siren in the distance.

"Sounds like the police are almost here," Olivia said. "I wonder how Dillon is doing."

Together, they jumped when there was a sharp knock on the truck door. "What is going on?" Asher called through the door.

"It's Asher." Billie rushed toward the door and opened it.

"Why does Dillon have some guy's face pushed into the ground?" Asher asked. He looked at Billie. "Hey, are you okay?"

"That guy out there accosted her," Olivia said.

Asher's face hardened. She had never seen him sport the look before, at least, not like that. He simply nodded at Olivia and headed back down the steps and away from the truck. Billie went outside and watched as Asher stalked down the boardwalk. She saw two Sea Glass Island police officers heading in the same direction.

"Turn him around," Asher said as he walked up.

"No, way, man," Dillon said. "You don't need any part of this."

"Turn him around," Asher said firmly.

"Asher," Dillon said, his voice held a warning.

Asher went around the men, and the minute Rob saw him, he held his fists in front of his face, ready for his approach. Without warning, Asher socked the man hard in the mouth.

"I want to press charges! This man just assaulted me," Rob shouted. Asher turned around and headed back to the food truck. Billie watched him, a little in awe. Though she disapproved of violence and retribution, seeing that play out felt nice.

"I think you should come on home with me," Asher suggested when he made it back to the truck.

"Yeah, you guys go," Olivia said. "The police are with them now and I used to work with these guys. If they have any questions for you, I'll send them your way."

"Thanks, Olivia." Billie stepped off of the truck. Asher put his arm around her and steered her away.

CHAPTER 8

Billie sat in her office chair and pushed her shirt to the side to check on her shoulders while Asher hovered.

"Are you okay? What happened out there?"

Billie nodded her head. "He was asking me all sorts of questions about Captain Stephens and the man in the net. He also told me that there's another man missing, a friend of his, who is also friends with the captain. He said none of them are 'good guys,' including himself and the captain."

"Who did he say was missing?" Asher asked.

"A man named Trevor Kaufmann," Billie said. "I have no idea who he is, and I still don't get why this guy decided to attack me. He insisted I knew more than I was telling him. And he has been watching us."

"Hmm, that name sounds a little familiar, but what do you mean by watching us? What makes you say that?" Asher asked.

"He knew we had spoken with Chief Abernathy last night, and that you and I are a couple." She shivered from head to toe."

"He's not going to be back," Asher said. "When the cops come to talk to us about what happened, I'll make sure he gets banned from the island."

"Can they do that?" Billie asked.

"I don't know," Asher said. "But one way or another, I'll make sure he never wants to return."

"I can't believe you hit him," Billie said. "You just walked right up to him and decked him."

Asher shook his head. "Between you and me, neither can I," he said. "I just went into robot mode."

"It was very gallant of you, but also very risky," she said. "I mean, don't get me wrong. I felt a great deal of satisfaction watching him go down."

Asher blushed slightly. He glanced down the hallway. "Here comes the chief," he said.

"Did you know his first name is Phillip?" Billie whispered.

"I did. Did you not?"

She shook her head. "That guy told me."

"Hello, Chief," Asher said, giving Billie a look.

"Didn't expect to see me again so soon, did you?" Chief Abernathy said.

Billie shook her head. "Not this fast," she said. "I suppose you're here to find out what happened."

The chief nodded his head. "Why don't we go out there and have a seat at one of the tables and talk?" He turned to Asher. "I already got a statement from two of my officers about your interaction with the man you just had a run in with. I will caution you not to add any more information than they already gave me. Understood?"

"Got it, Chief," he said. "I won't volunteer a single thing."

Billie stood up from her desk and followed the two of them down into the kitchen space. She took a seat in the seating area at one of the tables and waited while the chief settled into a seat across from her. Asher walked into the first kitchen area and started a new pot of coffee.

"Okay, Billie," Chief Abernathy began. "What did this guy say to you?"

"He grabbed onto me and held on pretty tight," she said. "He kept asking me questions about what happened out there on the fishing boat, and also wanted to know how well I knew Captain Stephens. He said that his friend was missing, and that he was a friend of the captain's."

"Did he give you a name?"

Billie nodded. "He said his name was Rob, and the missing guy was Trevor Kaufmann. He said Captain Stephens is a bad guy, just like him and his missing friend are bad guys."

"Anything else? Did he say anything about me?"

"He told me your first name is Phillip and that he had seen Asher and me speaking with you," she said, surprised by the question. "He'd been watching us and wanted to know what I told you. He sort of acted like you might not be a good person, either, Chief."

The chief nodded his head. "I see. Well, he is right about my first name," he said with a forced smile. "What did you say to him in response?"

"Just that I was on the boat when the body was discovered but I didn't see anything, and that I didn't know anything," she said.

"Okay, and did he say how long his friend had been missing?"

"Days, I think," Billie said. "No one has heard from or seen him in several days. And he was a friend of Jacob Stephens. That's what he said."

The chief nodded. "Okay, Billie. Thank you for speaking with me." He looked over at Asher. "I'd like for you two to let me know if anyone else comes around asking about me or any of this."

"Of course, Chief," Asher said. He set two coffee mugs on the table in front of them. "What do you think about this guy? Is he out to get your cousin or what?"

Chief Abernathy shook his head. "I… uhh, I can't be sure," he said. "But I'm not going to speculate, either. I have to be very transparent and very careful how I proceed with this investigation, given my relationship with the prime suspect in the other case."

"How is Captain Stephens now?" Billie asked.

"Well, he's out of jail," Chief Abernathy said. "I'm not sure how he posted bond, but he managed to and now he's out for a while. He's not supposed to come to the island or go off land, though."

"Why can't he come to the island?" Billie asked.

"It would be too easy for him to disappear," the chief said. "He has a sailing vessel and plenty of knowledge on how to stay gone for a very long time. It's standard procedure in a case like this." He sighed, stood up, and thanked Asher for the coffee, which he left untouched on the table.

"Why do I get the feeling the chief is a tormented guy right now?" Asher asked when he was gone.

"Because I think he is," Billie said. "I get the

feeling he's asking himself some hard questions about his cousin right now. He's definitely not acting normal."

"You don't think the captain is a bad guy just based off of what that thug out there said to you, do you?" Asher asked.

Billie shook her head. "I honestly don't know what to think about any of this mess," she said. She hesitated, sipped her coffee, and spoke again. "But there is something that is really bothering me."

"About what? The chief?" Asher asked quickly, his eyes wide.

Billie looked at him and hesitated a moment. "When we were on the boat, I heard a noise and felt the boat lurch, right?"

"That's what you said, yes," Asher agreed.

"Well, okay," Billie said. "I'm trying to work this out in my head. We heard the winch, or whatever you call it, lower the nets, right?"

"Right," Asher said.

"Why did we feel the lurch when the net was lowered and not when they were bringing the net up again?" she asked. "It seemed like the net was lowered and the lurch happened at the same time."

"I don't know what that means," Asher said. "What are you thinking?"

"I don't know yet," Billie said. "I'm not sure what any of it means, but something just doesn't add up about the timeline on the boat."

"Are you saying that you think the captain was involved?" Asher asked.

Billie sighed. "I don't know," she said. "But think about it. The captain might have looked disturbed, but we also know from what we found online, that he was in business with the victim."

"What do you want to do now?" Asher asked her.

"First thing I want to do is to go back to my house and take a shower," Billie said. "After that, I want to see what I can find out about A-1 Enterprises."

CHAPTER 9

With her hair wrapped up in a towel and Waffles secured outside near his luxury doghouse, Billie gazed out the window of her tiny house. She had a view of the water, even at a distance, and it offered her a sense of calm. After the terrible morning she had, any peace was welcome.

She removed the towel from her head and ran a brush through her hair before pulling it to the side and securing it in a loose braid. She glanced in the mirror, thankful how the shower had worked magic on her spirit.

Asher had reassured her to take her time. There was nothing especially pressing, though Billie had plans to check on Carl and the sushi truck around lunchtime. Rhonda had also promised to keep an eye on things for her from her community center storefront on the boardwalk.

Billie decided to take a slower approach to the rest of her day. She popped a coffee pod into her machine and retrieved her laptop from where it was charging in her bedroom. She glanced out the window at Waffles on her way back to the small table close to the kitchen. When the coffee was ready, she stirred in a little sugar and a generous amount of the creamer Enid liked to make for her own coffee and took a seat at the table. After the interaction she had with the stranger that morning, a little indulgence in some creature comforts felt like what she needed.

After a few healthy sips of her coffee, Billie opened up her laptop. There had to be something online that could help her understand more about what was going on. The fact that Sam had gone missing, and no one had heard from Trevor had to be related, especially since they were both involved with the captain in some way. She resumed her search for more information about the one link she had found between the fishing boat captain and the man found dead in one of his nets. She entered the name of the company as well as the names of both men.

At first, the search revealed the same information she had found before, including the name of the small town outside of Tampa where the company address could be found as well as where Jacob Stephens and Samuel Petrie were listed as owners.

This time, Billie decided to click on the "News" tab. Immediately, her search page was populated by a series of articles. The news articles had been published in a newspaper bearing the name of the small town. She clicked on the first headline that caught her eye.

"Dispute Halts Development of Three-acre Plot in West Hatton," the headline read. Billie scanned the article and wrote down the important details in the small notebook she kept in the kitchen. According to the article, five years ago, the owners of A-1 Enterprises appeared in front of the small town council seeking approval for the development of a storage facility. Billie recalled the other businesses she had found in her previous searches of Captain Stephen's business interests, including at least one other storage facility.

But the problem with the site in the small town of West Hatton centered on the amount of development the council required for the three-acre swath of land to be developed. City leaders wanted a new road created as well as adequate utilities installed. The pair, listed in the article as J. Stephens and Samuel

Petrie, appeared before the council for a second time. During this meeting, Stephens addressed the council with the idea of upgrading their project to a small apartment complex. The writer reported his comments as condescending toward members of the council when he declared that "With all of the investment you are attempting to wrangle out of us, we might as well up our own plans to recoup a greater return on said investment. Stephens's business partner appeared visibly upset and requested a recess from the meeting. Immediately, the pair stepped outside where a vigorous discussion took place after which both parties left the meeting without another word to the council."

Billie saved the article on her browser and returned to the list to scan more headlines. Development of the site began three years later, only to be abandoned sometime in the last six months. After several more articles, she had a clearer picture of the relationship between the two men. The question in her mind was whether or not a business disagreement could have ramped up to murder. And what about the second man who had gone missing? Was there any connection to the other man her attacker claimed was missing?

Billie sighed and rose to make a second cup of

coffee. It was the best she could do at the moment to keep herself awake and functioning when all she wanted to do was to retreat beneath her covers and sleep away the day. It was a stress response, and she had reached her stress limit already for the day.

When she returned to her seat and computer, a thought popped into her head. If the captain and his business partner had a public disagreement over the rental project, where did the business stand now? If the project had been abandoned within the past six months, maybe one of the two men had tried to buy the other one out. Or maybe the business had failed all together. She entered the company name once more into the search engine and this time included the word "bankruptcy." As far as she knew, most of the time bankruptcy claims were a matter of public record.

Sure enough, Sam Petrie had filed for bankruptcy on behalf of A-1 Enterprises just eight weeks ago. The captain's name was missing from any filings, and Billie wondered what that might have meant. Of course, bankruptcy meant angry creditors, and angry creditors could be motive enough for murder. Or possibly to frame someone for murder.

CHAPTER 10

Billie shut her computer down and rose to stretch her arms high over her head. She headed outside, knowing sunshine and sea air was what she needed most. Sitting around too long inside was not going to help her attitude or her mental health.

Waffles snored inside his doghouse when she walked past. It was just after lunch time, and she was determined to check in on her food trucks, and on Carl in general. The business with the body in the fishing net had taken up so much of her time and focus that she felt like she had not given him enough attention. As accomplished as he was as a sushi chef, he was a relative novice to the business side of things. She had little doubt about his ability to prepare the product, but the other nuances of business might overwhelm him fast.

Of course, while Dillon, Marcel, and the rest of the food truck managers were right there to pitch in when he needed advice, it was not on them to step away from their own businesses to help out if he got into trouble.

Billie crossed the festival grounds and headed for the gate to the boardwalk. She stopped just on the other side and gazed at the area already bursting with people. By noon, the boardwalk was usually fairly populated, but today, the size of the crowds resembled what she would have seen on opening day of a popular festival.

She headed straight for the shops first. Rhonda would be in her store fielding requests for information and maps of the area. Billie walked to the end of the row and pushed the door open.

"Well, hello there, sweetheart." Rhonda smiled. Three people stood in front of her. "I'll be with you in just a sec."

Billie nodded and walked to the large windows at the front of the store. She watched the crowds assemble around the trucks. From her vantage point, she could see several people gathered around the sushi truck. She was happy to see that the truck appeared to be a popular addition to the area.

"Billie, these folks here are from New York," Rhonda announced. Billie turned around and smiled at the man and two women accompanying him.

"Welcome to Sea Glass Island," she said, unsure what else to say.

"They were just complimenting the food down on the boardwalk," Rhonda continued.

"Especially the sushi truck," one of the women exclaimed. "We stopped there right before we came here, and everything was excellent."

"We really love the fact that some of the fish comes from local waters," the man added. "That's a very clever thing to do."

Billie understood the point of Rhonda's introduction and smiled. "That's terrific to hear," she said. "Thank you for sharing your thoughts."

"I told them that I'd never had sushi before I tried Carl's, and now I'm a convert," Rhonda explained.

The trio of tourists continued out of the store, leaving a few more compliments in their wake. Billie watched as they left and headed for the beach with a broad grin. "Thanks," she said. "I needed that today."

"Yeah, I heard you had a rough morning," Rhonda said. "How are you doing, honey?"

"You heard about it already?" Billie said. "Sheesh. Word does get around."

Rhonda laughed. "There's no shortage of tattle-tales on this island, but my informant made sure I knew because, well, because I look out for you. I know I'm never going to be Adeline, but I like to think I can keep an eye out for you anyway."

"I appreciate that thought, and the good intentions of your informant," Billie said. "But I have a feeling he left out his part of the entire affair."

"What part?" Rhonda asked. "What did Asher do?"

Billie smiled. Rhonda confirmed her suspicion that Asher was her unnamed accomplice. "He clocked the guy," she said. "Right in the mouth."

Rhonda laughed heartily. "Yeah, he left that part out," she said.

"Dillon deserves a lot of credit, too," she said.

"Asher mentioned that he was the one who pulled the guy away from you," Rhonda said. "I'm so glad to see you're okay. Did you come here to tell me that or was there something else you needed?"

Billie shook her head. "I just came to check things out down here," she said. "Unless you're free for lunch, then you can walk down there with me. Are you hungry? I really wanted to check in with Carl and see how things were going."

Rhonda grinned and glanced at the clock. "Well, it's just about lunchtime for me, so let me get my purse," she said and headed to the back of the store.

"Leave your purse here and lock up," Billie called after her. "You don't ever pay at the food trucks."

"I will pay and support your businesses," Rhonda said with a frown when she returned to the front.

"You're my official guinea pig," Billie said. "That comes with its perks."

Rhonda nodded and shoved her purse under the cabinet behind the reception counter. "Fine," she said. "But I'm in the mood for pizza today, if that's okay."

"Of course, that's okay," Billie said. "I'm not eager to eat the same things day after day either. Sometimes, tacos hit the spot. Other times, I can't stand to look at one just because that's what I smelled all day at work."

They headed down the walk toward the trucks. Billie counted ten people in line in front of the sushi truck. Carl caught her eye and smiled. He raised a gloved hand to wave at her. Clearly, everything was going well for him so far.

"Let's grab our lunch and sit on the beach," Rhonda suggested. She pointed to the pizza truck.

"As long as we can find a place to sit, sure."

"Right," Rhonda said. She stepped up to the order window and gave her order to Isa.

"Make it two," Billie said. "Put them both on my tab."

"Two Greek pies, personal size. Coming right up." Isa returned quickly with their lunch and sent them on their way so she could take care of her next guest.

"Shall we?" Billie headed toward the beach, happy to see a picnic table unoccupied.

"Traitor," Dillon called out to her from his truck window when he spotted the pizza in her hands.

"Where do you think I'm eating dinner?" Billie smiled when she called back to him. "I'll take a sweet tea right now though."

"Make it two!" Rhonda added.

Dillon nodded once and turned for their drinks. Billie ignored his antics and eyed her pizza. She hadn't eaten breakfast and her stomach growled in anticipation.

"I swear this is the best food on the entire island," Rhonda said as she leaned over her pizza and inhaled deeply.

"I sure hope you're including barbecue in that

assessment," Dillon said. He stepped out the door and handed out two sweet teas.

"Of course, I am."

"Better be," Dillon teased. He looked at Billie. "How are you doing, kiddo?"

"Doing better," she said. "Thanks for the drinks. And you know, for saving my rear this morning."

"Anytime," Dillon assured her before going back inside the truck.

"Looks like Carl is even busier over there now," Rhonda observed as they walked toward the picnic table.

"Do you mind stopping by after we finish?" Billie asked. "He seems to be handling things okay, but I want to make sure."

"Not at all," Rhonda said. She took a seat across the table from Billie and dug into her pizza.

When they finished, Billie gathered up the trash and stuffed it inside a nearby bin. The crowd in front of The Gulf Roll had thinned a bit, a perfect opportunity to check in with Carl. When she approached the truck, she was delighted to see the colorful display of sushi rolls. Unlike the other trucks, the interior was mostly stark white. Billie had worried about the ability to keep the white preparation counter clean, but the entire place looked spotless to her.

Carl had arranged the multicolor rolls on black platters in the covered display cases. The aesthetic was clean and modern, exactly what she would expect in a nice sushi bar.

"How are things going?" she asked as he worked. "Can I help with anything?"

"I'm doing great!" Carl looked up and grinned. "Busy," he said. "I've been hopping since I opened this morning."

"And how is the truck itself?"

His grin was even bigger. "It's amazing. The only issue I can see is the need to hire a part-time sous chef."

"Do you already anticipate the need for help?"

"Oh, yeah," Carl said. "I have a feeling we're going to need it, especially if today is an example of a normal crowd, not even a special occasion with an event on the island."

"He's right about that," Rhonda said. "It's a little busier than normal, but you just never know. It could be even busier than this any given day of the week."

"I'll leave that to you," Billie said. "If you feel like you need to hire someone, just run your plans by me and send our selected candidates over for a final interview. We'll both sit down with them and go from there. I can help out right now if you need me, though."

"I think I'm okay for today." Carl nodded. "There's one more thing I want to run past you."

"What's that?" Billie asked.

"It's the local seafood market I picked up today's catch from," he said. "The guy asked me if I was going to need a certain amount each day, each week, and so on. Well, I mentioned the fact that we planned to buy directly from Captain Stephens, depending on the outcome of his charges, and he told me that I might want to look somewhere else if I needed reliable delivery, it sure sounded like the captain wasn't too well-loved around there."

"He said all that?" Billie asked. "Did he say why?" She remembered the captain specifically saying he was friends with them there and they'd treat her right if she went, simply because of that.

"That was my next question to him. Stephens supplies the market, and Otto told me that his boat was shut down all of last week."

"Shut down?"

"Yeah, he didn't go out and do any fishing," Carl said. "I'll admit the guy was less than pleasant to talk with, but he seemed to be really upset about it. He said not only was he dealing with the shutdown, but his coworker was out of work, and he didn't have time to deal with even more issues. It sounded to me like the market has all sorts of problems going on. The guy even had his wife there yelling at him about working too many hours while he was trying to talk to me. It was crazy."

"Oh man." Billie hated to hear about a business having issues, but at that moment, she was more concerned with why the captain would shut down. "Did he say why the captain didn't go out?"

"Rumor has it, the captain wasn't able to go out because he's not always able to pay for the fuel in his boat or for his crew."

"Wow," Rhonda said. "That's not good news."

"Okay, why don't you ask around and see if you can find another supplier?" Billie suggested.

"You might want to keep your voices down," Rhonda whispered. "The captain is right there and walking in this direction."

Billie looked up. Rhonda was right. The captain was walking casually toward them.

"How's the sushi selling?" he asked when he stopped in front of them. "I wanted to come down here and check in to see how things were going."

"Things are great here. How are you doing?" she asked awkwardly.

Captain Stephens shoved his hands into the pockets of his pants. "I take it you heard about my unfortunate misunderstanding. I was able to post bond while they work this nonsense out."

Billie swallowed hard. "I was under the impression you weren't able to visit the island," she said, unsure why she'd even said it.

Captain Stephen laughed and nodded his head. "You heard right, but that's before I appealed the decision and got permission," he said. "I think it helps to have a close relative in law enforcement. They know my cousin isn't about to let me get away with anything."

"I'm sure he won't," Rhonda said. "Billie, if you'll excuse me, I have to get back to work."

Billie bid her goodbye and turned back to the captain. "Chief Abernathy said they were afraid that you might be a flight risk, given the nature of your job," she said, looking around and feeling comfortable enough to talk since she was in a public place.

"Maybe so, but if I take off, I'll lose the money I posted for bond, and the house I put down as collateral," he whispered with a wink to her. "You know, I heard from the chief that you had an ugly interaction this morning."

She felt a slight bit of relief that he mentioned the

situation and wondered how he had money for bond but not fuel for his boat. She wanted to bring it up but didn't know how. "I was accosted by a stranger asking a lot of questions about you and some other man he said you knew."

"Phillip said the police took the man into custody. Do you remember anything about him? What he looked like or what he said his name was?"

"He just said his name was Rob, and I honestly don't remember much, except that he was a really big man," she said.

"Asher said you were hurt by him," Carl piped up and said.

"He hurt you?" the captain asked.

"I was a little red, but I'm okay now."

"I'm sorry he did that to you," the captain said. "But you don't remember anything else?"

"You could talk to Dillon," Carl volunteered. "He's down there at the barbecue truck. He's the one who took the guy down."

Captain Stephens nodded. "You're sure it wasn't one of my crew members, right?"

Billie shook her head. "No," she said quickly. "I didn't recognize him at all."

The captain exhaled slowly. "Okay, I just wanted to make sure," he said, then lowered his voice. "If you ask me, there's someone on the crew everyone needs to watch carefully. Tyler Parker, the young guy the two of you met. I think he's up to something and I wouldn't be surprised if he was involved with Sam's death somehow. He's apparently not been very forthcoming with me about a few things, and I'm told he has a bit of a gambling problem."

Billie said nothing. She glanced at Carl, who was equally stone-faced.

"Anyway, I wanted to check in with the two of you," Captain Stephens said. "As soon as I get back to my boat, I'll be in touch to see what we can do to fill your orders. Sound good?"

Billie nodded her head and forced a smile. "Can't wait, Captain." With that, he tipped his hat and turned back the other way.

CHAPTER 11

"Do you believe him?" Asher asked her later that night. They were seated inside the commissary kitchen.

Asher had three platters on the table in front of him. He eyed the barbecue platter Dillon had prepared for him with great expectation. Another platter of tacos and sushi was next to it, along with leftover cupcakes from the mousse truck.

"The captain? I'm not sure," Billie admitted. "I met Tyler Parker on board, and he seemed like a normal young man. But the captain seems like a good guy, too. At least I thought so until I heard what that Rob guy had to say."

"Have you looked this Parker guy up in one of your internet searches?"

Billie shook her head. "Not yet," she said. "I don't know where to look. How do you even find out if someone has a gambling problem? I want to look up Trevor too, actually. I think there might be something there. Oh, and I'd like to figure out if there's another reason why the captain shut his boat down."

"What do you mean?" Asher asked.

She explained to him what Carl had told her and waited while he stared off into the distance for a moment. "That's where I recognized his name," Asher said. "There's a Trevor who works at the fish market."

"Are you serious? How can we find out if it's the same guy? Is there a website with their names or something? I bet it's the same guy and that's how he knows the captain!" Things were starting to make more sense. The guy at the fish market had told Carl his coworker hadn't been at work, and Trevor hadn't been heard from for days. That couldn't be a coincidence.

"Calm down a second," Asher said. "We're going to think this through just as soon as I get some food in my stomach."

"Fine." Billie sighed. She picked a California roll up from the platter and took a bite.

"So far, those are my favorite," Asher announced.

He picked a second roll up and popped it into his mouth.

Billie finished off her roll and nodded. "I think he uses real crab, but it's the fresh cucumber and avocado for me."

"Do you feel like a walk down by the marina after dinner?" Asher asked her. "I thought we could check out the new boat together. We can talk more about the case too."

"You mean the one you want to move into?" Billie said a little aggressively. She definitely wanted to talk about the case but had to admit the whole Asher buying a boat thing had her feeling very curious.

"That's the one," Asher said. "We didn't have a chance to finish the discussion we started about it."

"A walk sounds like fun," Billie said. "Maybe if I end the day with a good walk, it will help undo the memory of the terrible walk from earlier. How about I take Waffles out first and then we can go to the marina together after?"

Asher finished off the barbecue platter and began to load the dishes into the dishwasher in one of the kitchen areas while Billie returned to her tiny house to take care of Waffles.

Shortly after, they met at the marina. The winds

were calm, and the air held a slight chill, perfect for a long-sleeve shirt and a walk. Billie was happy to be out and about, but despite the fact that she was with Asher, she still found herself looking over her shoulder.

"I heard he's in jail on the mainland," Asher said when they reached the beach.

"What are you talking about?" Billie asked. She didn't want to engage in a conversation about her fears.

"You're looking around at everything as if you expect the bogeyman to jump out at you at any minute," he said.

Billie sighed. "I'm trying not to think about it," she said.

"He really did a number on you, didn't he?" His face reddened slightly. "I should have hit him on top of the head until he was buried up to his neck in sand."

"I think you made an impact when you hit him in the mouth. You did hit him pretty hard."

"I really did." Asher chuckled uncomfortably. "And he did go down."

Billie laughed. "Okay, I feel better now," she said.

They continued toward the marina. The sunset glowed in hues of pink and orange over the gulf.

Billie sighed and wrapped her arm around Asher's. She was happy when he leaned in closer. "I bought the boat so we could spend some time out on the water together," he said at last.

"That sounds like a lot of fun," Billie said.

"I've always wanted to live on the water," Asher continued.

"I can see the appeal," she said. "I do wonder why you want to get rid of the fifth wheel, though."

Asher cleared his throat. "I'm going to sell it," he said.

"To buy the boat?"

"No," Asher said with a grin. "I'm going to sell it so I can buy a tiny house from Nolan, just like you did. He's going to custom make it for me and I'll get my wish to live on the water until it's done."

Billie stopped. "You've ordered a tiny house? That's awesome!"

"Yeah," Asher said. "Nolan and I are designing a full-sized kitchen in it, too. I am so excited about it!"

"You know you live next door to a commissary kitchen, right?" Billie teased.

He wrapped his arm around her waist and tickled her as she walked. Billie laughed out loud. She looked up and noticed someone walking down the beach straight for them. "Who is that?" she asked, suddenly not laughing.

"Looks like the chief," Asher said. He released her waist.

"Chief Abernathy," Billie called out when he approached. "Are you out for a walk this evening?"

"I was actually on my way over to the festival grounds to speak to you," the chief said. His ordinarily ruddy complexion was bright red from the exercise.

"What's going on?" Asher asked.

Chief Abernathy caught his breath. "We just got word that Trevor Kaufmann was found severely beaten and near death."

"I thought he was missing," Billie said. She felt a cold chill run through her.

"He was missing, but he was found this afternoon," the chief said. "Someone called in a tip about a homeless guy sleeping at some old building. Turns out, he wasn't homeless. When the sheriff's department checked it out, they found Trevor."

"Do they know what happened to him or who hurt him?" Billie asked. Her mind was spinning.

The chief shook his head. "We aren't sure yet, and he's unable to talk to tell us anything. He's got a broken jaw. But they did find something rather interesting with him. Maybe even a little disturbing if you ask me."

"What did they find?" Asher asked the question Billie was afraid to.

"They found a photograph on his phone of what looks to be a body in the water, and also an uncashed check in his pocket from my cousin Jacob for ten thousand dollars," the chief said.

"A body? You mean Sam's? Asher asked.

"Was it a personal check?" Billie wanted to know.

The chief nodded. "We don't know yet whose body it was or if it even was a body. And yes, it was a personal check for business consulting fees," he said. "But there was also another thing, a handwritten diagram of the *Fin So Fast*."

"Your cousin's boat," Asher stated what everyone already knew.

"It is his boat," the chief said. He shook his head again. "I don't know anything more unfortunately. I can't understand why he had that information on him, and I can't get a straight answer about why the there was a check from my cousin for such a high amount."

"Especially when the captain's boat was shut down last week because he couldn't afford the fuel to take it out and fish," Billie said. She considered the bond money too but left that part out for now.

"Who told you that?" Chief Abernathy asked.

"Carl, my sushi truck manager, was told that by the guy who works at the fish market down at the marina," Billie explained.

"None of this adds up." Asher ran his fingers through his hair and groaned.

"Actually, I think things are beginning to add up," Billie said. "But I'm worried the final answer is going to be something none of us want to hear."

CHAPTER 12

"What about what Captain Stephens told you about that kid on his boat?" Asher asked Billie. They continued their walk toward the marina. The police chief joined them as they quickened their pace.

"You spoke to Jacob?" the chief asked her.

Billie nodded as she walked. "He was down on the boardwalk around lunch time. Rhonda and I went down there for lunch."

"Are you saying you saw my cousin there?"

"I did," Billie confirmed. "It was right after Carl told me what he had heard about the captain's financial woes. Captain Stephens made the remark that he was concerned that Tyler Parker might have had something to do with Sam's death. He also insinuated that Parker might have a gambling problem."

"Tyler? I don't think that's true," Chief Abernathy said. "I don't know what Jacob is talking about, but the Tyler I know has been saving since he was sixteen for a fishing vessel of his own. He wants to captain his own vessel and crew someday."

Billie stopped walking for a moment and stared at the chief. "Are you sure about that?"

Chief Abernathy nodded his head. "I'm completely sure," he said. "Tyler grew up on Sea Glass Island, just like I did. His parents went to school with Jacob and me."

Billie sighed and stared off into the distance. The sun had almost dipped below the horizon. They didn't have much daylight left. "Chief, can you get us on board the *Fin So Fast*?"

"Can we even get near it?" Asher asked. "I mean, it was part of a crime scene."

"The investigation regarding the boat is complete," the chief said. "Not that the powers that be are very forthcoming about sharing what they found with the local police department or anything. I actually think Sam's death is a lower priority to them than some of the other cases they are working on."

"Like what?" Asher asked.

"Like drugs and other smuggling operations," the chief answered. "Those cases they loop me into from time to time, but the case of a dead body found on a local fishing vessel, not so much."

"Maybe that's because their prime suspect is a member of your family?" Asher suggested.

Chief Abernathy shook his head. "I guess you haven't heard," he said. "They've completely withdrawn the charges against Jacob."

"Withdrawn? Is that different from dropped?" Asher asked.

"Withdrawn was their wording, meaning that they don't have enough evidence to support the charges right now, but they might file them again if they do," the chief said. "They're now looking into Trevor as a possible suspect."

"Chief," Billie cut in, things beginning to come together in her mind. "You haven't answered my question. Can you get us on board?"

"I'd rather you tell me why you want to go on board," he said. "I don't know what your reasons are, so maybe it's better if you tell me and I can go on board myself if need be."

"Do you think the captain will be there?" Asher asked.

"I don't know," Chief Abernathy said. "As far as I know, Jacob was supposed to be on the mainland today tying up some loose ends on a business development he has outside of Tampa."

Billie glanced at Asher but said nothing about what she knew about A-1 Enterprises. "I just need a minute or two on the boat," she said. They reached the marina and crossed the parking lot toward the boat slips.

"The *Fin So Fast* is just down the way toward the far end," the chief said. "Because of its length it's one of the last boats on the left side. I'm going to ask you again to tell me why you want access."

Billie said nothing as they made their way down the wooden walkway toward the boat slips. She looked out for any sign of the captain. When they made it to the far left end of the marina, Chief Abernathy stopped in front of the boat. She had not paid much attention to the vessel since her fateful ride, but she was shocked by the mere size of it. The rigging arms had been secured upright in order to make the boat fit.

"Is it possible to drop the nets while the boat is docked?" Billie asked.

"I think you can raise and lower the nets on board, but you need to be at sea before you can drop them," Chief Abernathy said. "Why?"

"Because I have a thought and I want to see if I

am correct," she said. "Can you work the lever yourself?"

"I think so," the chief said. "It's just a matter of raising and lowering it. You stay there." He walked toward the control panel on the back of the boat's cockpit. "You just want me to lower the lever?"

Billie nodded. "Without actually dropping the net, of course," she said.

Chief Abernathy pushed a switch in the middle of the panel down for three seconds, then abruptly stopped. Billie listened to the soft whir of the small motor that worked the lowering arm, then indicated for the chief to raise it again a second later. Again, she could hear the whir of the motor.

"Is that all?" Asher asked.

"Is what all?" Captain Stephens asked. He stood in the doorway that led to the steps into the hull of the boat. "What are the three of you doing here?"

"Following up on a suspicion I had," Billie said boldly. Having the chief with her made her feel much braver.

"What are you doing here, Jacob?" Chief Abernathy asked. "I thought you were supposed to be on the mainland."

"I had a few other things to do," Jacob said. "You still haven't told me why you're here."

"Are you getting ready for a long trip, Captain?" Asher asked. He pointed to a pile of wooden crates stacked up on the stern. "Looks like you've got enough food there to last for six months out at sea."

"I'm refilling the cupboards down below," Captain Stephens said.

"Is that all you're doing?" the chief asked. "Why are there three suitcases on the deck next to the crates of food, Jacob? And don't tell me that isn't your personal luggage. I bought that set for you the day you bought this boat."

"Get out of here," Captain Stephens shouted. "I don't have to answer your questions!"

"Actually, you do," the chief said.

"How about me? I have a question for you," Billie said. "Why did you pay Trevor ten thousand dollars to kill your business partner? Was it around the same time he filed for bankruptcy?"

Captain Stephen's face paled. "You have no idea what you're talking about, young lady," he sneered. "I suggest you get this woman out of here, Phillip."

"What are you talking about, Billie?" Asher asked.

She kept her eyes on the captain. "Isn't it true that you thought Sam's body was going to be long gone before you set sail again after a week of being shut down? I think you paid Trevor to kill your partner, only he had another idea in mind."

"You have no idea what you are talking about," Captain Stephens said again. "I'm not going to warn you another time! Get out of here." He headed into the cockpit, but the chief stopped him.

"It wasn't until you told us what you thought about Tyler Parker when things started adding up for me," she said. "You planted some real seeds of doubt about him, things you knew not to be true, given your family's connection to his parents. You were trying to place the blame on him, just like Trevor was hoping to do."

"Okay, but that doesn't prove that he killed anyone," Asher said, not helping at all.

"I don't think he killed anyone," Billie continued. "Isn't that right? I think you paid Trevor to kill Sam, which he did, but I also think he planted the body in your net, so you'd get in trouble for it. I think you weren't as friendly with the folks at the fish market as you claimed you were. I think you're high and mighty attitude is what got you into this mess in the first place."

"I said get out of here," the captain huffed.

Billie shook her head. "All this would explain why Sam's body was found in the net on board this boat instead of at the bottom of the gulf where you expected him to be. The picture they found with Trevor, they weren't sure if it was a body or not." She looked at the chief. "It probably wasn't, but it was meant to look that way, I bet. I think Trevor told you he dropped Sam in one place, and that's why when you took Carl and me out on the water, you went to a different place then usual, right? Because you didn't want to accidentally come across Sam."

"You are absolutely out of your mind, lady," Jacob hissed. "Trevor killed Sam and it had nothing to do with me. I'm the good guy in all of this. It's because of me you're going to have a local catch on that truck of yours. You should be happy with that, not trying to cause me grief."

"So, you admit you know that Trevor killed Sam, then?" Asher asked, eyes wide. "It's the same Trevor who works at the fish market, too, isn't it?"

He pushed his captain's hat up on his head and stared hard at Billie.

"There you go," Billie said, pointing toward him. "That's the same look you had on your face when you discovered Sam's body in the fishing net. You weren't shocked to see him dead, you were just shocked to see him there."

"Oh, Jacob," Chief Abernathy said. He stood in

front of him and pulled out his phone, quickly typing something on the screen. He glanced at Asher and flashed the screen at him.

"Hey, Chief, when you're on the phone, you might want to check to see if it was Otto from the market who beat up Trevor. I hear they were having some issues over there." She stared back at the captain. "You know, the funny thing about small town newspapers? They report every little scandal that happens during their civic meetings, like the public falling out you had with Sam in West Hatton over the three-acre land development deal. Sam wanted to keep things simple, but you were determined to make it a bigger, better project. You pushed it until the money ran out, and then Sam filed for bankruptcy before you knew what he was doing."

"Is all of this true?" the chief asked, looking between his cousin and Billie.

"She knows nothing," Jacob said. "I had a little business trouble with Sam, but I never would have killed him over it."

"No, you just paid someone else to do it," Billie said. "Except, Trevor wasn't your biggest fan. So, he went through with the deal for the money, but he wanted you to get caught more than he wanted anything else. So, he took a fake picture for your benefit." She looked at the chief. "Your cousin shut down operations for a week and let the rumor fly it was because he had money troubles, a narrative that would match up when the bankruptcy was discovered."

"Only you did that just to give it time for Sam's body to be long gone from where you thought he was," Asher chimed in.

"And when you spotted the body in the net, the first thing you did was pull out your phone and double check the photo Trevor had sent you," Billie said. She turned to the chief. "I bet they let him go in part because Sam's body had never been in the water. He wasn't pulled up in the net. He was in the net when the captain went to drop it. That's why the boat lurched forward when he worked the controls, just as you did a few minutes ago. Only, the motor didn't whine as loud that time and the weight of the body wasn't there to cause the boat to shift slightly."

"I've heard enough," Captain Stephens shouted. Chief Abernathy turned around to face his cousin after having been listening to Billie. But instead of just his cousin, he turned and found himself staring down the barrel of a gun. "You and your curiosity got you into this mess. And now you're going to have to pay for it. Unfortunately for me, that means a member of my own family is going to have to pay the price as well. For that reason, I am going to make sure I drop you overboard into a school of sharks, alive."

"You don't have to do this, Jacob," Captain Abernathy said. His hands were raised to his shoulders.

Jacob snickered and rolled his eyes. He motioned for Billie and Asher to get on the boat. "You are familiar with the cabin below deck. The three of you can await your fate there, out of my way. If you think about running, I'll shoot."

"I don't think that's necessary," a deep voice called behind them. Billie turned her head to see Rob, the guy from the grounds, standing behind them. Two women in business suits flanked him on either side.

"What is this?" the captain demanded.

"You better put your gun down, Jacob," Chief Abernathy said, lowering his hands. "This guy is known as a jerk in the field, but he is a dead shot. He won't tell you twice, and he won't miss."

CHAPTER 13

Billie held an ice pack to her head. She reclined her lounge chair back and stared up at the stars overhead. "I can't believe that man was a federal agent," she said.

"Undercover guys sure do some interesting things," Asher said. "But I think there's much more to the scope of his case against Captain Stephens than just murder. Maybe it's a good thing this all played out the way it did."

"More than just murder?" she asked, raising up a little to look at him. "What is there that makes murder 'just murder?'"

"An entire smuggling operation that puts thousands more lives in jeopardy," he said. "I know that answer is crass and disappointing, but when you went down on the deck of the boat, Agent Robert Barnwell explained it very quickly to me. I had no idea who the chief was asking me to call when he showed me his phone screen or what for, but I'm glad I did."

"I can't believe I passed out," Billie said. "If it wasn't for this massive headache, I wouldn't believe it at all." She rolled her eyes under the ice pack.

"I can't believe I punched a fed," Asher muttered. "I'm so glad I didn't get in trouble for that."

"That whole thing was insane. With the way he acted, there was no way to know he was a cop. He really made me think he was involved in all of this."

"That was probably the point, and I guess that means he's good at his job." Asher shrugged.

"But why was he even asking me questions in the first place. It's not like I was involved in some way."

"Because he saw the chief talking to us. In the beginning, they thought the chief might have been trying to protect his family. Not only was he far away from the case because they were related, but it was also because there were some questions posed about the chief himself."

"Like he knew more than he was letting on?" Billie asked. "No way. Chief Abernathy is a good guy."

"I know that, but they didn't, and they had to be

sure. You just happened to be the unlucky soul who was in the wrong place at the right time."

Billie chuckled. "Well, isn't that great? What did the chief say? Is he mad they were trying to accuse him of something?"

"I think he's a little annoyed, but he knows how the job works," Asher said. "I'm pretty sure he's more concerned with you, though."

"Me?"

"The chief thinks you passed out from the shock of everything. Seeing Rob, Robert… Agent Barnwell wearing a federal badge," he said. "He felt bad knowing what went on between you and the agent, and yet he couldn't tell you who he really was. He said, not only was he upset because they believed him to be involved and brought you into it, but also because they weren't sure what you might have accidentally heard on that boat, and they couldn't be too careful about how things played out."

She held anger toward the agent, even if he was trying to protect more than just her. "I don't want to be mad, but I can't help it."

Asher nodded. "The chief knows you're going to be angry with him and I don't think he's looking forward to facing you. I bet he's glad he's busy with the mess over at the fish market right now. You were right about Otto. He was working all these extra hours and his wife was furious about it. Imagine when he finds out the reason why Trevor was missing work was because he was busy plotting someone's death?"

Billie pulled the ice pack down and shrugged. "Oh boy." She chuckled. "Well, I can't be angry with him," she said. "He was doing his job, and for crying out loud, he just put a member of his own family away. You heard what he said about Jacob. They grew up like brothers. I don't have much to be proud of in my own family, but that would be hard."

"Yeah, I guess we know that from what happened to Isa with her mom," Asher said.

"That's for sure," she said. "My head hurts."

"I know," Asher said. He reached over and patted her leg and then sat back up. He glanced toward the commissary kitchen. "I know this might not be the right time to bring it up, but what do you say we take the boat out next weekend? We can take a little cruise toward Urchin Island and spend a couple of nights away."

"Do we have any events this coming weekend?"

"No," Asher said with a slight chuckle. "Do you ever check your event calendar?"

"I hit my head." She laughed, remembering she'd just looked at it not that long ago. "Leave me alone."

"What do you think, Billie? Maybe it's too soon for us to go away together, but I think it would be fun. And there are two sleeping areas in the cabin."

"I do think it would be fun," she said.

"But?"

"But I'm worried about leaving when the sushi truck is so new," she said. "And Carl is so new, and it isn't very often that we have all of the trucks in operation at once when I'm not around to help."

"You do know that you are going to have to appoint someone to be in charge when you can't be, right?"

Billie grinned. "Yeah, that's what I have you for," she said.

"Come on, Billie," Asher said. "I'm trying hard to make an effort here. I don't want this relationship to just stay casual and silly. I want to build something with you."

"What do you want me to do?" she asked. "I'm happy to hear you say that, but I'm scared to leave the trucks alone for too long. That isn't a statement about us, Asher. It's about me trying to be responsible for the business my grandmother left to me."

"I understand that," Asher said. "But you can also learn to delegate and manage your managers."

"I'll ask again. What do you suggest I do?" Billie asked.

"Put Dillon in charge and pack your bags." Asher grinned. "You're a smart woman, like I said. If you can solve murders as well as you do, then you're certainly smart enough to know you can leave him in charge.

Billie pursed her lips together and nodded slowly. "Dillon would be the best candidate for the job," she said. "Do you really think I could get away?"

"I think you better try," he said. "The 'S.S. Scullery Maid' is going to need you on her maiden voyage."

"Please tell me you didn't name your boat the 'Scullery Maid,'" Billie said flatly.

"Why? Is there something wrong with naming the boat after you?"

Billie cackled and slowly rose from her seat and walked around behind him. She opened the plastic bag filled with melting ice and dumped it over his head.

***

If you enjoyed Control Your Tempura and are looking for more food truck adventures, preorder Friend or Froze, today!

AUTHOR'S NOTE

I'd love to hear your thoughts on my books, the storylines, and anything else that you'd like to comment on—reader feedback is very important to me. My contact information, along with some other helpful links, is listed on the next page. If you'd like to be on my list of "folks to contact" with updates, release and sales notifications, etc.… just shoot me an email and let me know. Thanks for reading!

Also…

… if you're looking for more great reads, Summer Prescott Books publishes several popular series by outstanding Cozy Mystery authors.

CONTACT GRETCHEN ALLEN

Visit my website for more information about new releases, upcoming projects, and be sure to check out my special Members Only section for extra freebies and fun!

Website: www.gretchenallen.com

Email: contact@gretchenallen.com

Visit the Summer Prescott Books website to find even more great reads!

Made in the USA
Coppell, TX
06 May 2023